I'm Heading to the Rodeo

by **Emmi S. Herman**

illustrated by
Claire Louise Milne

Bebop Books

An imprint of LEE & LOW BOOKS Inc.

I'm waking up early
for school today.
But in my mind . . .

2

3

I'm heading to the rodeo.

I'm brushing my hair
until it flies away.
But in my mind . . .

I'm patting the golden
mane of my horse.

"Finish your breakfast. Can't be late,"
Mom calls out from the door.
But in my mind I hear . . .

"Barrel race!"
and the rodeo crowd roars.

It's bump after bump in the pickup truck
as dust begins to rise.
But in my mind . . .

I'm riding a steer,
the seconds ticking by.

All at once the truck stops short
and Mom lets out a shout.
"The corral gate is open.
The colt and goat are out!"

I grab some rope
from the back of the truck
and race up to the colt.

I jump right on
and ride with speed
to meet the frightened goat.

Just like in the rodeo
I tie the rope and then . . .

I herd the goat into the pen,
to safety once again.

I'm on the road to school today.
My heart and body soar.
'Cause in my mind the rodeo . . .

is closer than before.